ALFRED GOES TO THE LAND OF FUN

Written by
Shandel-Elton

For my cousins – Kathryn, Daniel and Ryan. The memory of reading you bedtime stories is one I hold dear to my heart and will treasure always.
And my beautiful niece, Tahlia for whom I hope this story will be a constant delight.
But most importantly, for my parents who nurtured a passion for storytelling in me as a young boy curious about the world and everything in it!

Published in association with
Bear With Us Productions

© 2021 Shandel-Elton
Alfred goes to the Land of Fun

The right of Shandel-Elton as the author
of this work has been asserted by him in
accordance with the Copyright Designs
and Patents Act 1988.
All rights reserved, including the right of
reproduction in whole or part in any form.

ISBN: 978-1-7399097-0-3

Cover design by Richie Evans
Design by Luisa Moschetti
Illustrated by Biva & Mai

www.justbearwithus.com

Illustrated by
Biva & Mai

ALFRED GOES TO THE LAND OF FUN

Written by
Shandel-Elton

There once was a man named Alfred
who lived in the Land of Scrum,

He loved having adventures,
and scratching his bum.

One morning after eating his breakfast
of hot porridge and plum,
He decided to visit his cousin Jane in the Land of Fun.

Together they could fish by the river
and sail paper boats,
Climb trees, fly kites and watch the grazing goats.

With peanut butter sandwiches,
fried bacon and apple juice,

Alfred packed his bag, grabbed his
coat and put on his boots.

Out the door he went,
on his journey out of town,

Into fields and meadows,
then the forest beyond.

There were flowers, squirrels
and trees,

Birds of many colours,
butterflies and bees.

A pond where he could rest

And feed the ducklings
waddling from their nest.

For miles and miles, he dragged his feet,
Until finally he stumbled upon a street.

Without a moment to lose he began to run,
Maybe this street led to the Land of Fun.

Around the corner and over a bridge,
He arrived at what looked like a tiny village.

The houses here were very odd;
Shaped like triangles and covered in green mud

They had triangle windows and triangle doors,
With triangle chairs on the triangle floors.

Could this be one of the three Triangle towns,
Ruled by pixies wearing triangle crowns?

Suddenly there was a loud pop in Alfred's ear.
He screamed loudly and jumped up in the air.

A little pixie had sneaked up on him.
She pointed and laughed, as he rubbed his chin.

"Oh, silly! That was the sound of my bubble gum pop!
I have endless flavours like coconut,
pineapple and banana berry,

Grape, orange, lemon and even cherry!
You can find many more in the Land of Gum.

Would you like to try some?"
"Yes, please! My favourite is plum."

"Follow me, sir, I know just the place,
Bertie's shop has them by the case!"

She buzzed on ahead down a cool, grassy lane,
Until they came to a sign shaped like a candy cane.

Welcome to the Land of Gum!
Already this looked better than the Land of Scrum.

Land of Gum

There were so many bright colours and hues,
It smelled sweeter than any perfumes.

Anyone would be lucky to live here,
Alfred thought.
They could have gum of any flavour and of any sort.

Very soon they were near the shop,
But something made Alfred stop

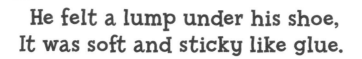

He felt a lump under his shoe,
It was soft and sticky like glue.

When he looked down, he saw what was there,
He had stepped in gum, it was everywhere!

The streets were littered with gum of all different colours,
To clean this mess, it would cost millions of dollars.

Alfred hopped carefully on clean bits of ground,
To avoid touching the sticky gum all around.

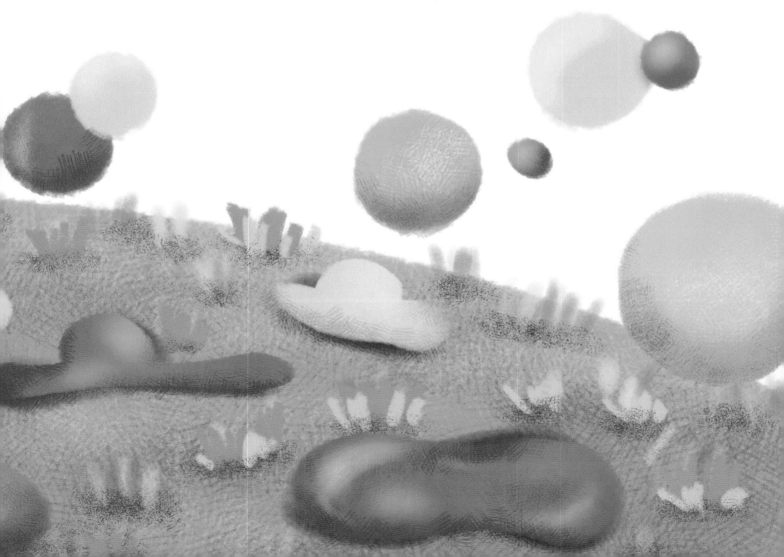

When he was at the shop,
        he bought some plum gum from Bertie,
And waved the pixie goodbye
        before his shoes continued to get dirty.

One, two, three steps out the shop.
Four, five, six towards the hilltop.

Alfred made his way out of the town and into the Red Wood.
It would be a shortcut if he walked as quickly as he could.

The Red Wood was filled with red trees that had red fruits,
Even the little plants that grew sent out only red shoots.

Everything you could see was coloured red,
And after a while it began to hurt Alfred's head.

Using his bag as a pillow and making a blanket from his map,
He decided to lie down and take a quick nap.

Soon Alfred drifted off to sleep,
Snoring loudly and sounding like an old jeep.

Several hours went by, and day turned into night.
But Alfred awoke with a terrible fright.

He dreamt that some strange creature was eating his shoe,
And woke up to find it was indeed true!

He opened his bag, pulled out a flashlight,
And turned it on, letting it shine bright.

There, a wandering goat lay at his feet,
Staring at him with shoelaces hanging from its teeth.

Give me back my shoelaces, you thief.
Instead you can chew on this red leaf!"

With his laces safely in hand,
Alfred resumed the journey he had planned.

All through the wood there was silence, no sound,
Only darkness and cold air all around.

This is scary, Alfred thought,
If there were monsters here, he would definitely be caught

Frightened of what he might find up ahead,
Alfred climbed into a tree in sheer dread.

There he would wait until sunrise,
Staying awake and never closing his eyes.

When the sky slowly began to fill with light,
Alfred was overjoyed at the view that came into sight.

He could see buildings glistening in the sun,
Just ahead was the Land of Fun!

All he had to do was take ten steps forward,
If only he hadn't been such a coward!

In an instant he was down the tree,
And entered the Land of Fun in utter glee.

He zoomed past the huge playground, the
circus and Ferris wheel,
A large rollercoaster and a
rainbow-coloured building made of steel.

Through the markets and into the square,
He raced to the house of his cousin Jane Ear.

When he was finally there,
he knocked anxiously on the door.

"I wonder if she'll recognise me?"
He wasn't sure.

Patiently he waited,
but no one was in the house.

JANE ♥

He pressed his ear to the door;
But inside was as quiet as a mouse.

Suddenly a man
came strolling by,

It was Jane's neighbour,
Mr Bumblefly.

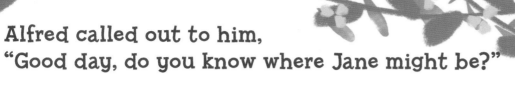

Alfred called out to him,
"Good day, do you know where Jane might be?"

"Oh, I'm sorry, lad,
she left this morning, sometime around three."

"When will she be back, do you know?"

"I think maybe a week from tomorrow.

She said that she was feeling
a little sad and glum

So, she decided to visit her cousin Alfred
in the Land of Scrum!"

The End.

Printed in Great Britain
by Amazon